Chicka Chicka Boom Boom

LITTLE SIMON

New York   London   Toronto   Sydney   New Delhi

by Bill Martin Jr
and
John Archambault

illustrated by
Lois Ehlert

For Arie Alexander Archambault, new baby boom boom —JA

For Libby and Liza, Helen and Morris —LE

LITTLE SIMON

An imprint of Simon & Schuster Children's Publishing Division

1230 Avenue of the Americas, New York, New York 10020

Text copyright © 1989 by Bill Martin Jr and John Archambault

Illustrations copyright © 1989 by Lois Ehlert

This Little Simon edition 2013. Also available in a Simon & Schuster Books for Young Readers

hardcover edition, an Aladdin paperback edition, and a Little Simon board book edition.

LITTLE SIMON is a registered trademark of Simon & Schuster, Inc.,

and associated colophon is a trademark of Simon & Schuster, Inc.

For information about special discounts for bulk purchases, please contact

Simon & Schuster Special Sales at 1-866-506-1949 or business@simonandschuster.com.

The Simon & Schuster Speakers Bureau can bring authors to your live event.

For more information or to book an event contact the Simon & Schuster Speakers Bureau

at 1-866-248-3049 or visit our website at www.simonspeakers.com.

Manufactured in The United States of America 1012 LAK

10 9

ISBN 978-1-4169-2718-1

ISBN 978-1-4424-3891-0 (eBook)

Chicka Chicka Boom Boom

A told **B**,
and **B** told **C**,
"I'll meet you at the top
of the coconut tree."

"Whee!" said **D**
to **E F G**,
"I'll beat you to the top
of the coconut tree."

Chicka chicka boom boom!
Will there be enough room?
Here comes **H**
up the coconut tree,

and **I** and **J**
and tag-along **K**,
all on their way
up the coconut tree.

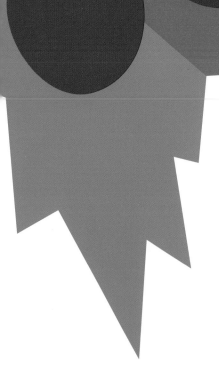

Chicka chicka boom boom!
Will there be enough room?
Look who's coming!
L M N O P!

And **Q R S!**

And **T** **U** **V**!

Still more—**W**!
And **X Y Z**!

The whole alphabet
up the—Oh, no!

Chicka chicka...
BOOM! BOOM!

Skit skat skoodle doot.
Flip flop flee.
Everybody running to the coconut tree.
Mamas and papas
and uncles and aunts
hug their little dears,
then dust their pants.

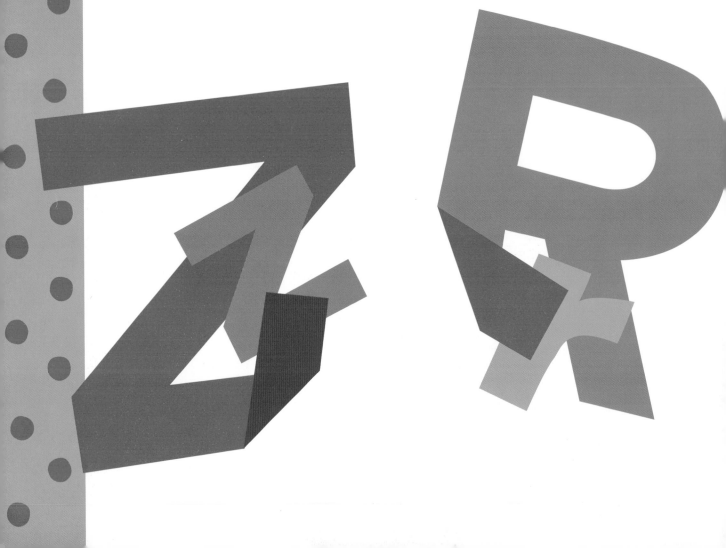

"Help us up,"
cried **A** **B** **C**.

Next from the pileup
skinned-knee **D**
and stubbed-toe **E**
and patched-up **F**.
Then comes **G**
all out of breath.

H is tangled up with **I**.
J and **K** are about to cry.
L is knotted like a tie.

M is looped.
N is stooped.
O is twisted alley-oop.
Skit skat skoodle doot.
Flip flop flee.

Look who's coming!
It's black-eyed **P**,
Q R S,
and loose-tooth **T**.

Then **U** **V** **W**
wiggle-jiggle free.

Last to come
X Y Z.
And the sun goes down
on the coconut tree...

But –
chicka chicka boom boom!
Look, there's a full moon.

A is out of bed,
and this is what he said,
"Dare double dare,
you can't catch me.
I'll beat you to the top
of the coconut tree."
Chicka chicka
BOOM! BOOM!

cDdEe
hliJjKk
nOoPp
sTtUu
xXYyZz